See the Ghost

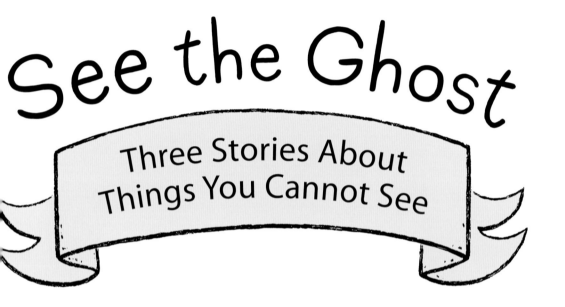

Three Stories About Things You Cannot See

David LaRochelle

illustrated by Mike Wohnoutka

CANDLEWICK PRESS

Story Number One

See the Ghost

See the ghost.

See the ghost
scare the dog.

See the ghost
scare the cat.

See the ghost
scare the flowers.

Wait a minute.
Why aren't these
flowers afraid?

Maybe I'm not
scary anymore.

See the ghost
look in the mirror
to see if he is
still scary.

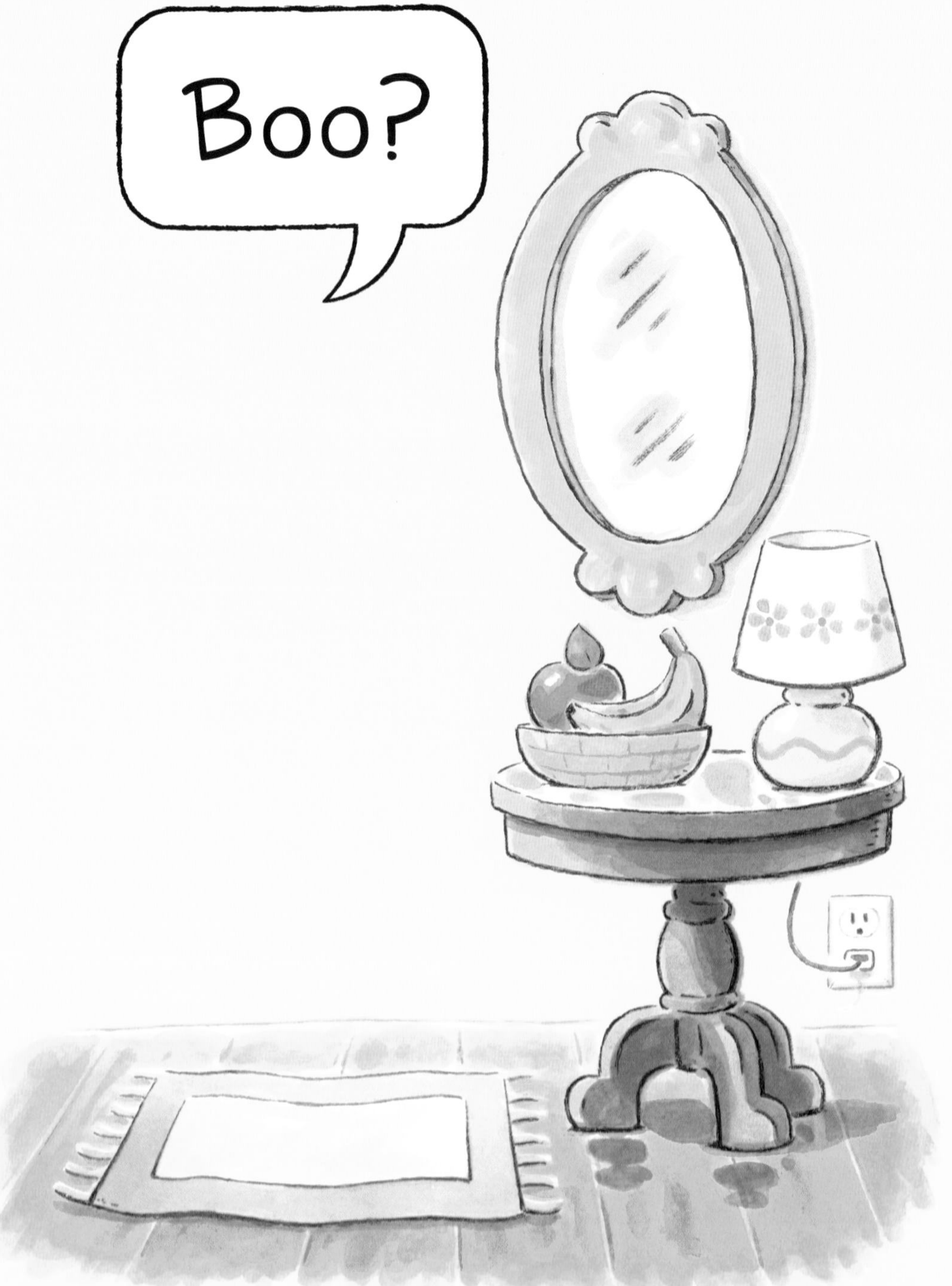
Boo?

See the ghost
hide under the table.

Story Number Two

See the Wind

See the wind
blow the leaves.

See the wind
blow the leaves
off the page.

See the wind
blow the dog
off the page.

See the wind
blow the cat
off the page.

See the wind

blow

the

words

whoosh!

off the page.

See the wind
blow the leaves
and the dog
and the cat

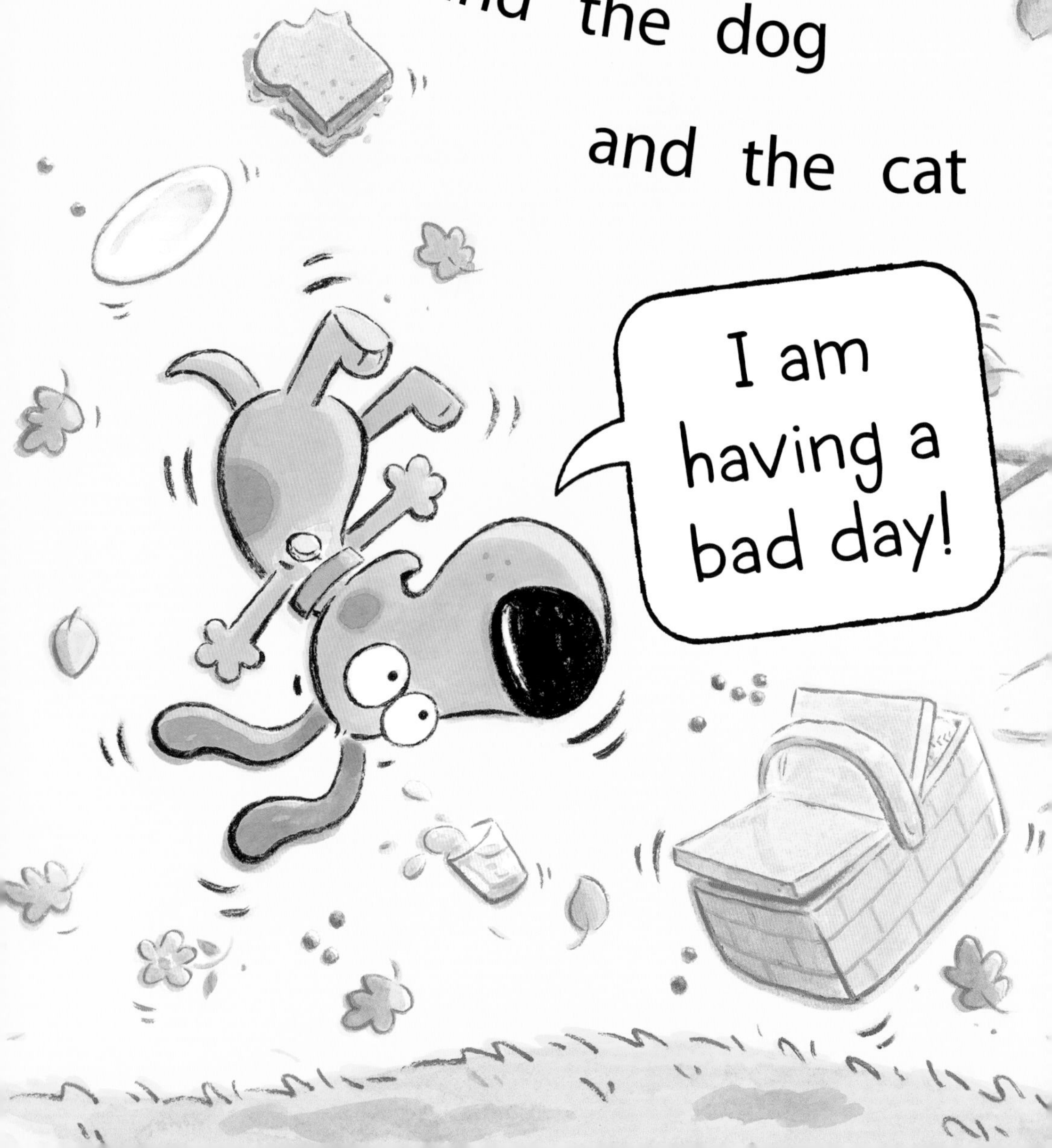

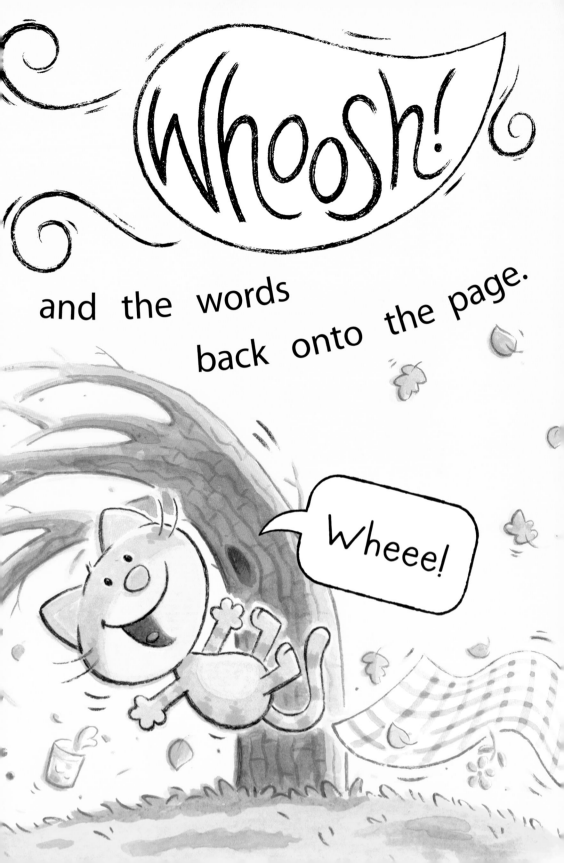

Whoosh!

and the words back onto the page.

Wheee!

See the wind
enjoy a picnic
with the dog and cat.

Story Number Three

See the
Fairy

See the fairy.

See the fairy
wave her magic wand
at the dog.

See the fairy
wave her magic wand
at the cat.

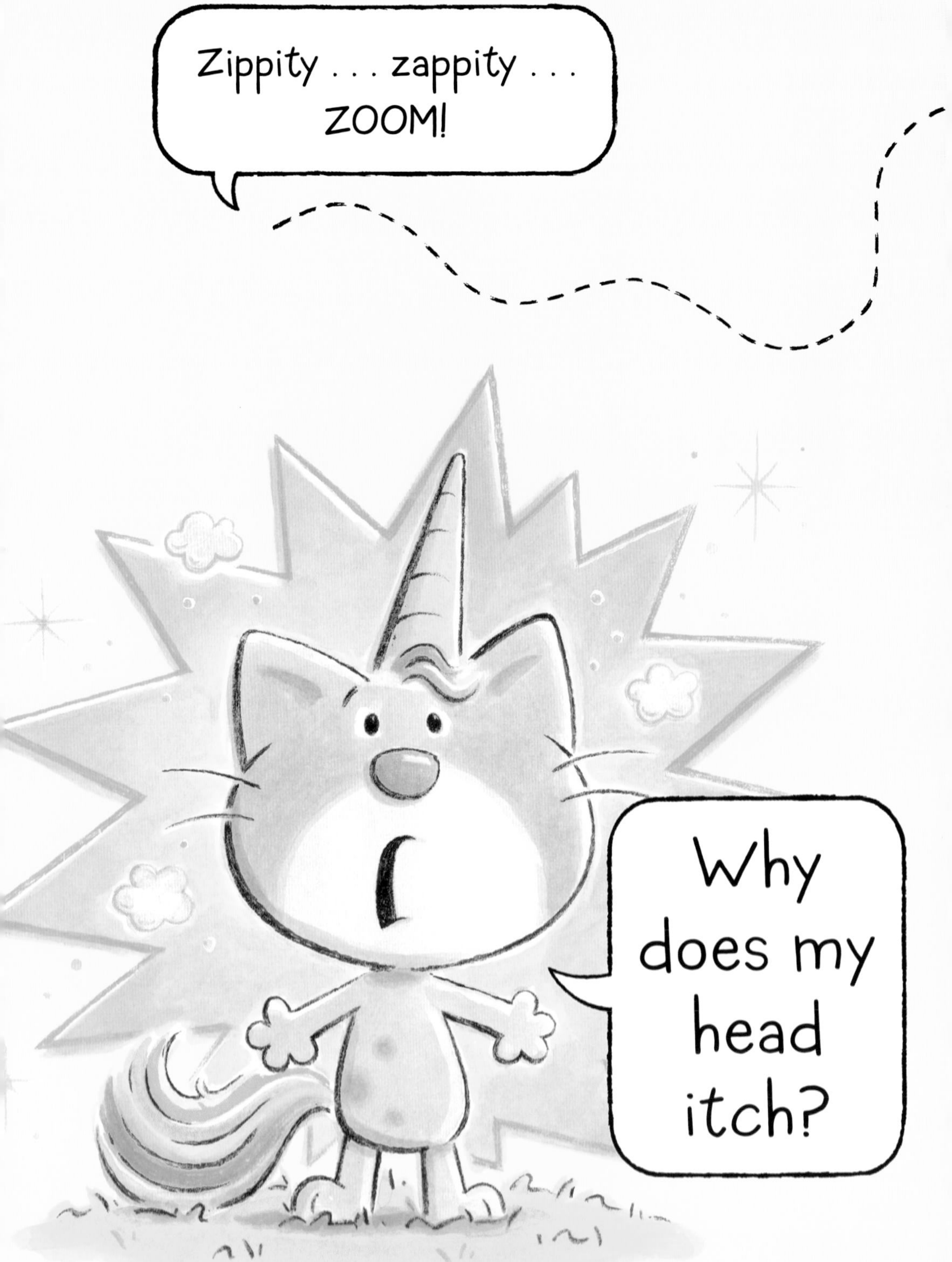
Zippity . . . zappity . . . ZOOM!
Why does my head itch?

See the fairy
wave her magic wand
at the ghost.

See the fairy
wave her magic wand
at the wind.

Okay, okay. You made your point.
If I fix everything, will you let me back into the book?

See the fairy
wave her magic wand
one last time.

See the dog,
the cat,
the ghost,
the wind,
and the fairy
spend the afternoon
together.

To my good friend Mike Wohnoutka
DL

To Lauren Pettapiece, thank you for
all your magic behind the scenes
MW

Text copyright © 2023 by David LaRochelle
Illustrations copyright © 2023 by Mike Wohnoutka

First edition 2023

Library of Congress Catalog Card Number 2022907139
ISBN 978-1-5362-1982-1

23 24 25 26 27 28 CCP 10 9 8 7 6 5 4 3 2 1

Printed in Shenzhen, Guangdong, China

This book was typeset in Myriad and Coop Forged.
The illustrations were done in gouache.

Candlewick Press
99 Dover Street
Somerville, Massachusetts 02144

www.candlewick.com